P9-ARC-858

For Margaret...

Timothy and Gramps

Ron Brooks

Bradbury Press
Scarsdale, New York

Library of Congress Cataloging in Publication Data

Brooks, Ron. Timothy and gramps.

SUMMARY: After his grandfather's visit to his classroom,
Timothy enjoys school more.
[1. School stories.   2. Grandfathers—Fiction]
I. Title.
PZ7.B7986Ti   [E]   78-17389
ISBN 0-87888-139-5

Gramps always took Timothy to school
in the mornings, and home again
in the afternoons.

Timothy didn't like school much.
He had no brothers or sisters,
and he had no special friends,

except for Gramps.

They went on walks together.

Gramps told Timothy stories,

and Timothy told Gramps stories.

But at school
Timothy played mostly by himself.

In the mornings, for Show and Tell,
other children had pets to show to the rest of the class,

and stories to tell about things
they had done with friends.

Or sometimes they just brought something
they had found, and talked about that.

But Timothy had no pet of his own and he could never seem
to find anything special enough to bring and show.

But once or twice,
Timothy asked Gramps
if he would stay
a little while.

He wanted to talk about his grandfather,
but he couldn't decide quite how to begin.

Gramps didn't know what to say either.
He just said "Good morning . . .",

and then he went home.
But he gave it some thought.

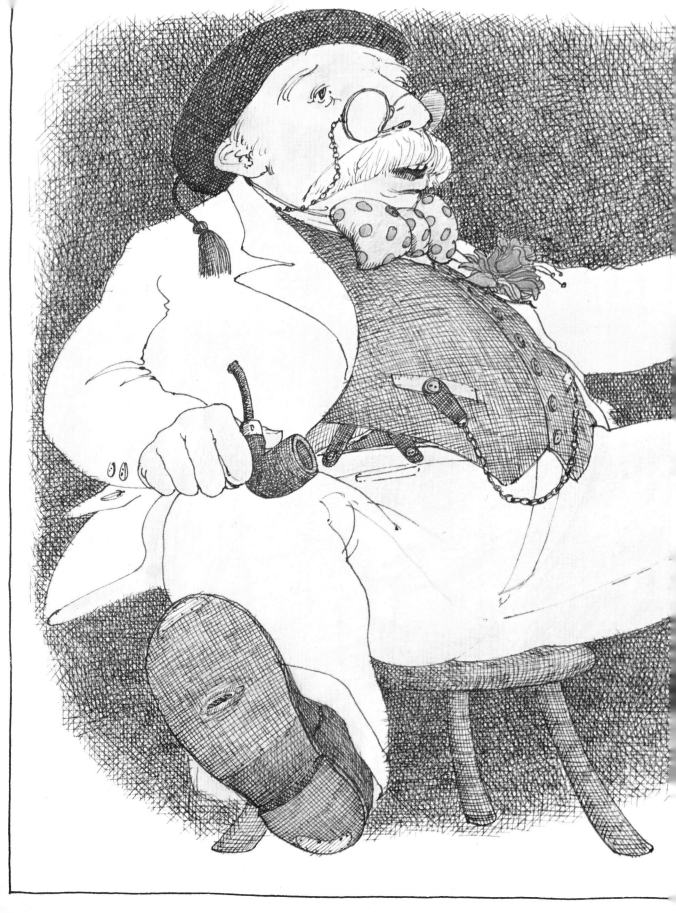

And the next day, came back.
Much to everyone's delight, he sat down,
and told them all a good long story.

After Gramps had gone, all the other children
crowded around Timothy and asked him to tell
them more about his Grandfather.

And, after a while . . .

Timothy did.
He told them Gramps's own, special story.

From then on,
school didn't seem half so bad.